Diseases and Disorders of Youth

Kids and Autism

Kris Hirschmann

ReferencePoint Press®

San Diego, CA

ReferencePoint Press®

For more information, contact:
ReferencePoint Press, Inc.
PO Box 27779
San Diego, CA 92198
www.ReferencePointPress.com

LIBRARY OF CONGRESS CATALOGING-IN-PUBLICATION DATA

Name: Hirschmann, Kris, 1967– author.
Title: Kids and Autism/by Kris Hirschmann.
Description: San Diego, CA: ReferencePoint Press, Inc., 2019. | Series: Diseases and Disorders of Youth | Audience: Grade 9 to 12. | Includes bibliographical references and index.
Identifiers: LCCN 2018005897 (print) | LCCN 2018006004 (ebook) | ISBN 9781682823965 (eBook) | ISBN 9781682823958 (hardback)
Subjects: LCSH: Autism in children—Juvenile literature. | Autistic children—Juvenile literature.
Classification: LCC RJ506.A9 (ebook) | LCC RJ506.A9 H57 2019 (print) | DDC 618.92/85882—dc23
LC record available at https://lccn.loc.gov/2018005897

Contents

Introduction

A Global Epidemic

When Amy was three and a half years old, her mother, Cheryl, noticed a pattern of alarming behavior emerging. "She was extremely verbal; however, she wasn't interacting with the other kids at her preschool very much. . . . She also had huge problems with transitions or with anything else that didn't go her way. She'd have huge tantrums, often over little things,"[1] Cheryl recalls.

As Amy's behavior worsened, Cheryl became concerned enough to seek advice from the school's psychologist. The psychologist did not see anything unusual during a one-on-one meeting with Amy. But Cheryl persisted. "I insisted she observe my daughter at her preschool with her peers . . . [and] that's when my world changed,"[2] she says. Following an in-class observation, the psychologist diagnosed Amy with autism—a disorder of the brain and nervous system that can affect a person's cognitive, communication, social, and physical skills in a wide variety of ways.

A Global Epidemic

Amy's story is far from unique. It is repeated many thousands of times each year—up to a hundred times per day in the United States alone, according to one estimate. It strikes youth of every ethnic group, although its incidence is higher among Caucasians than African Americans, Hispanics, or other ethnicities. Worldwide, the disorder affects youth in all cultures and regions, making it a truly global epidemic.

The scope of this epidemic has only been fully recognized in recent decades. According to a 2014 study released by the Centers for Disease Control and Prevention (CDC), 1 in 68 American children—about 1.5 percent of the population—now has autism. In 2000 the number was thought to be 1 in 150 children. The incidence of autism increased between 6 percent and 15 percent each year from 2002 to 2010, making autism the world's fastest-growing developmental disability. Today an estimated 3.5 million Americans have autism. Globally, the number is thought to be about 1 percent of the human population, which works out to about 76 million people as of 2018.

On the Rise?

Scientists have mixed opinions about the apparent rise in autism. Some feel that it is a matter of great concern and may reflect the environmental impacts of a changing world. Many studies have attempted to find links between autism and the environment. So far, however, the results of such studies have been largely inconclusive.

Many other scientists feel that the rising incidence of autism is largely an illusion. They believe that the recent growth in autism diagnoses has more to do with increasing awareness than any real change in numbers. They point out that medical professionals are catching the disorder earlier and more often. Public awareness, too, plays a role. "As people become more aware of the term autism over time, it's causing parents to have their kids be examined more often,"[3] explains scientist Stefan Hansen, who authored a major study of more than 675,000 Danish children. Published in 2015, this study found that at least 60 percent of Denmark's increase in autism diagnoses was caused by a change in the diagnostic criteria for the disorder.

Prevalence of Autism Spectrum Disorder

The most recent available data from the Centers for Disease Control and Prevention breaks down the incidence of autism in American children by sex and race. The data shows that autism occurs much more often in boys than girls. It is most common among white children and least common among those of Hispanic descent.

Prevalence of Autism Spectrum Disorder (ASD) in 8-year-olds (2012)

		About 1 in every "x" children
Overall		**1 in 68**
Sex	Boys	1 in 42
	Girls	1 in 189
Race	White	1 in 65
	Black	1 in 76
	Asian/Pacific Islander	1 in 88
	Hispanic*	1 in 99

*All other groups are non-Hispanic.

Source: National Institute of Mental Health, "Autism Spectrum Disorder (ASD)," April 2016. www.nimh.nih.gov.

Researcher Paul Shattuck of the University of Wisconsin–Madison agrees. He points out that the autism diagnosis has absorbed other disorders, particularly in the areas of mental retardation and learning disabilities. "Many of the children now being counted in the autism category would probably have been counted in the mental retardation or learning disabilities categories if they were being labeled 10 years ago instead of today,"[4] he explains. Indeed, graphs of intellectual disability versus autism diagnoses clearly show that in the United States, at least, a drop in levels of the first diagnosis corresponds quite neatly to a rise in the second.

The Debate Continues

To nonscientific members of the public, however—and particularly to upset parents of autistic children—this type of number crunching can seem unsatisfying and unconvincing. As autism figures have risen, so has the vocal criticism of alleged autism triggers, such as vaccines, environmental toxins, and more. This narrative, which has been spearheaded by public figures such as actress Jenny McCarthy, fans the flames of a difficult topic and keeps the debate raging in the public arena.

Scientists generally take a cooler, calmer approach. Still, many refuse to reject the basic ideas expressed by angry parents. They feel that rising awareness explains some of the rise in autism, but not all, and they think that it would be a mistake to look the other way on this issue. "These factors alone don't account for the entire increase in autism prevalence reported over the past two decades," says scientist Michael Rosanoff of Autism Speaks, an autism awareness and advocacy organization. "It's vitally important that we conduct research that teases out the effects of diagnostic changes on changes in autism prevalence over time to understand the factors that are truly causing a rise in autism."[5]

> **"It's vitally important that we conduct research . . . to understand the factors that are truly causing a rise in autism."[5]**
>
> —Michael Rosanoff, scientist at Autism Speaks

The CDC and other organizations worldwide are carrying out this type of research. Autism will probably never disappear from the human population; it is too widespread. But it is likely that scientists will find at least some answers over the coming decades. With more knowledge, there is real hope that humankind will find new and better ways to cope with this global disorder.

Chapter 1

What Is Autism?

Six-year-old Alex cannot speak, and he will not make eye contact with anyone, including his mother and father. He bangs his head against the wall repetitively, and he smears his own bodily waste everywhere when he gets the chance. He bolts from the house if the doors are left unlocked. If his parents try to stop Alex from doing these things, he becomes agitated and throws violent temper tantrums.

Nine-year-old José spends most of his time obsessively lining up toy cars in his bedroom. The cars have to be in a particular order that never varies: first the red one, then the blue one, then the yellow one, and so on. When José is not lining up the cars, he is talking about them to anyone who will listen. He especially loves to talk about his cars over dinner, which is identical every night: eight chicken nuggets and fifteen French fries with ketchup. If the food or the numbers are wrong, José will not eat.

Fourteen-year-old Raina is an exceptional student with an unusual talent for mathematics. She is attractive and outgoing. However, she has trouble making and keeping friends. She always seems to say the wrong thing in social situations, and she feels somehow out of step with her peers. No matter how hard she tries, she just cannot seem to fit in.

These three children are very different, but they have something in common. They all have autism. This disorder affects an estimated

1.5 percent of all American youth (and presumably adults as well, although many remain undiagnosed) and about 1 percent of the population worldwide. Despite the millions of people this includes, the disorder is still not completely understood. But scientists have made a great deal of progress in learning about and defining autism.

Defining Autism

Autism is a neurodevelopmental disorder. This means that it relates to the development of the brain and nervous system. In autistic individuals, something goes wrong during the development process, so the brain and nervous system are structured and operate in atypical ways. This does not mean autistic people cannot function. They can, sometimes very well. But their brains are wired differently than the norm. This physiological difference affects the way a person perceives and responds to the world.

One writer with autism gives a vivid analogy that describes how this works. She asks readers to imagine an autistic person's neurological wiring as a frayed stereo speaker cable:

> At one point we're positioned so that the things of life are coming through clearly and we may almost seem OK. . . . Then the wire wiggles and begins to produce some static—and we become confused and stressed because we're trying to hear the "tune" of our surroundings over and against the torture of the snap, crackle and pop of the crimped cord. Suddenly the wire is *all* static and we're utterly undone—because the racket is just too much to bear and we're suffering from the neurological distress.[6]

The exact physiological differences and impacts of this faulty wiring vary from person to person. For this reason, the symptoms of autism also vary widely. However, some symptoms are more common than others. Autistic individuals generally have trouble with social communication and interaction. They tend to have

It can be difficult to identify autism. The specific symptoms vary from person to person, and are often not visible.

restricted patterns of behavior, interests, or activities. They often have noticeable physical tics, such as a habit of hand flapping, difficulty making eye contact, or a lurching walk. They also tend to lack physical coordination and often struggle with athletics. Together, these symptoms paint the classic picture of autism.

Autism Is a Spectrum

Saying autism has a classic picture, however, is a bit like saying all redheads look the same. It simply is not true. The specific symptoms of autism vary for every person. As professor and autism expert Stephen Shore famously puts it, "When you have met one person with autism, you have met one person with autism. Everyone is different."[7]

> "When you have met one person with autism, you have met one person with autism. Everyone is different."[7]
>
> —Stephen Shore, professor and autism expert

This variation is the reason autism is more correctly referred to as autism spectrum disorder (ASD). In physics, a spectrum is a range of all the colors that are visible to the human eye. The spectrum begins with deep red and moves through shades of orange, yellow, green, blue, indigo, and violet to form a rainbow. Within this range, there are millions of possible color points. In the same way, the autism spectrum can take endless forms.

For the parents of newly diagnosed youth, this variation can be overwhelming. There is no one-size-fits-all instruction manual or source that explains the disorder and lays out, step by step, what to do about it. Each family must learn the ins and outs of their own child's autism—a process that can be very confusing and may take years of trial, error, and help from specialists to navigate.

Types of Autism

The term *autism spectrum disorder* is not just a handy descriptive phrase. Since 2013 it has been the official term for any form of autism, regardless of its severity. This diagnosis appears in the latest edition of the American Psychiatric Association's *Diagnostic and Statistical Manual of Mental Disorders*, or DSM-5 for short. In the book's previous edition, autism fell under the broader heading of pervasive developmental disorder, or PDD, and included several subtypes. The diagnosis was altered after research showed that the subtypes could not be reliably distinguished from one another. In casual usage, however, laypeople and professionals alike still use the old categories to distinguish different autism presentations.

A subtype called autistic disorder is what most people think of when they hear the word *autism*. The most common type of ASD, it usually emerges before three years of age. It is characterized by strongly impaired development, including significant problems with social interaction and communication and restricted, repetitive behavior. Children with autistic disorder have little or no interest in other people, to the point that they are sometimes said to be living in their own world.

Children with an ASD subtype called Asperger's syndrome are not as significantly impaired as those with autistic disorder. These children have normal verbal and intellectual abilities—in fact, they often score in the above-average range on intelligence tests. They are able to connect and interact with other people to varying degrees. But like children with autistic disorder, they also have social problems and a limited scope of interests.

Children whose symptoms do not quite fit either of the previous two descriptions may be put into a catch-all category called PDD-NOS, which stands for pervasive developmental disorder, not otherwise specified. PDD-NOS is also called atypical autism because it matches some of the criteria for autism but not all. It is usually thought of as being milder than autistic disorder, but this is not always the case. Some characteristics may be milder, but others may be more severe, so PDD-NOS can pose a significant challenge to people with this diagnosis.

The fourth and final subtype of autism is called childhood disintegrative disorder (CDD). In CDD, children develop normally for at least two years and then suddenly lose some or most of their communication and social skills. This is an extremely rare disorder, and there is some debate among mental health professionals about whether it is part of the autism spectrum at all. Whatever its root cause or classification, however, the symptoms of CDD are undeniably similar to those of autistic disorder.

Higher and Lower

In a rainbow, the word *spectrum* refers to a range of colors. In the context of autism, this word refers to a range of function—one's life skills and abilities. Individuals with better cognitive, communication, and social skills and fewer quirky behavior patterns are

Autism vs. Autistic

There is an ongoing debate in the autism community about the appropriate use of the words *autism* and *autistic*. Advocates of what is called identity-first language believe that it is fine to refer to someone as being autistic. In this view, saying "my autistic child" implies that autism is the child's neurological identity. It cannot be changed, and it is a part of them. Acceptance of this fact equals acceptance of the child.

The competing view is strongly in favor of what is called person-first language. In this view, it is more appropriate to say "my child with autism." By placing the child before the disorder, the speaker implies that the disorder does not define the person. Rather, it is an afterthought—something the child has but which is not the most important part of his or her identity.

Although autism organizations are increasingly adopting the use of *autistic*, there is no right or wrong answer to this question. Experts in the field suggest that people pick the label that feels right for them and their families while respecting the views of others. By asking people about their preferred words and then using them, supporters of both views can live in peace with each other.

said to be higher functioning. Those with Asperger's syndrome fall into this category. A similar unofficial term, *high-functioning autism* (HFA), refers to individuals whose abilities and behavior resemble Asperger's syndrome but who showed an early language delay and generally were diagnosed much earlier in life. HFA individuals, too, are well able to manage most demands of daily life.

The opposite end of the autism spectrum is referred to as being lower functioning. Low-functioning individuals may have significant impairments in many areas of life, from communication to cognition, social skills, and physical coordination. They may need a great deal of help from family and medical professionals to navigate the world. Those with autistic disorder fall into this category, as do those with CDD.

Individuals with PDD-NOS have a wider range of function. Depending on their symptoms, they can fall at either end of the spectrum or anywhere in between.

> **"There is a very wide range of possible outcomes [in autism]. . . . For an individual child, the outcome may be knowable only with time."[8]**
>
> —Dr. Thomas Insel, former director of the National Institute of Mental Health

The terms *higher-functioning* and *lower-functioning* are very commonly used by all manner of people involved with autism in any way. They are well understood and accepted. However, these terms are not precise—there is no test or scale that measures a person's level of functioning. And researchers point out that the level may change over time. "There is a very wide range of possible outcomes," says Dr. Thomas Insel, former director of the National Institute of Mental Health. "For an individual child, the outcome may be knowable only with time."[8]

Emerging Autism

Although things do change with time, the behavioral symptoms of ASD often appear early in a child's development. Many children show such symptoms by twelve to eighteen months of age or even earlier. The National Institute of Child Health and Human Development lists five red-flag behaviors to watch for in infancy. They include problems with eye contact, no response to the child's own name, problems following another person's gaze or pointed finger to an object, poor skills in pretend play and imitation, and problems with nonverbal communication. Any of these behaviors should alert caregivers and medical providers to the possibility of autism.

Many parents are not aware of these early signs. Often they do not start worrying until a child fails to start talking at a typical age. After this point, though, the signs and symptoms of autism become increasingly obvious. Also, as a child with autism gets older, developmental gaps widen between the child and his or her peers. By age six, it is usually clear whether a child falls somewhere on the autism spectrum.

Autism and Intelligence

An organization called the Autism and Developmental Disabilities Monitoring Network tracks and compiles data on children with autism around the United States. It reports that based on IQ scores, a little over 50 percent of autistic children are either intellectually disabled (defined as IQ of 70 or less) or borderline disabled. The rest are average or above average in intelligence.

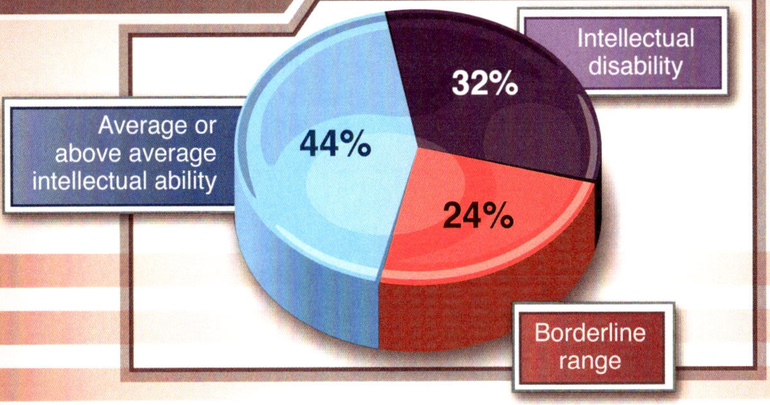

Source: Autism and Developmental Disabilities Monitoring Network, "Community Report on Autism 2016," 2016. www.cdc.gov.

Communication Problems

Communication problems are a hallmark of autism. These problems vary widely from one child to another. Some children with severe ASD cannot communicate using speech or language at all. Others have very limited language skills. Some have rich vocabularies but only when discussing specific subjects of interest. Still others understand speech as well as anyone but feel no need to respond to it. They ignore people who talk to them and may not react to their own names. When they do feel like interacting, however, many of these children have the ability to "turn on" and function appropriately.

Many children with autism, particularly those with high-functioning autism or Asperger's syndrome, do have excellent language skills. However, even these children show patterns of language use that are noticeably different from the norm. One

Autism and Life Expectancy

In 2016 the first major study of autism and life expectancy was released. Published in the *British Journal of Psychiatry*, the study tracked about twenty-seven thousand Swedish adults with autism over a twenty-two-year period. It compared this group to 2.6 million people without ASD. During the study period, 1 percent of the nonautistic population died—but a shocking 2.5 percent of the autistic population passed away. Breaking these numbers down further, researchers discovered that the life expectancy for the general population was about seventy years. In the ASD group, that number fell to fifty-four years, on average. For those with cognitive disabilities, the outlook was even bleaker, with an average life expectancy of just thirty-nine years.

Researchers suggested many possible reasons for these numbers, starting with the many known ASD-related health problems. Epilepsy, which affects 20 percent to 40 percent of people on the spectrum, is known to impact life expectancy. In addition, heart conditions often arise in autistic adults, perhaps due to the stress of daily life with autism.

This stress has another major impact. Researchers found that suicide is a leading cause of death among people with ASD, particularly for those without cognitive disabilities and most notably for females with Asperger's syndrome. In this population, suicide rates were nine times higher than in the general population. "We need to look at what we can do to improve the quality of life for people with autism," said autism expert Steve Silberman in response to these findings. "The cost of not doing so is death."

Quoted in David Mills, "Why People with Autism Die at a Much Younger Age," Healthline, March 25, 2016. www.healthline.com.

example is a tendency to say things that have no meaning or that do not relate to the conversation they are having with others. For example, a child might count or recite the alphabet over and over. Or, when asked how his or her day was, the child might respond with completely unrelated information. Some children also have a habit of repeating things that are said to them. This condition, called echolalia, can be immediate (when the child repeats things someone has just said) or delayed (when the child repeats things heard at an earlier time).

Autism can also affect a child's tone of voice and manner of speaking. Some children on the spectrum speak in an unusually high-pitched or singsong voice. Others speak in a monotone, without normal up-and-down inflection. Still others talk haltingly and are unable to maintain a typical verbal flow. Even if the conversational content is appropriate, the manner of delivery is clearly different from that used by neurologically typical, or neurotypical, children.

Behavior Patterns

Certain behavior patterns are also typical of autism. Repetitive behavior, as it is known in the field, is one of the most revealing characteristics. Children on the spectrum may constantly flap their arms or hands, flick their fingers outward, bang their heads, or rock their bodies back and forth. They may obsessively jump, spin, and twirl. They may also use objects repetitively; for example, by flicking a rubber band, playing with a piece of string, opening and closing a door, or rubbing their fingers against a favorite piece of textured fabric. This behavior is sometimes called "stimming," which is short for self-stimulating.

Narrow interests and obsessions are also common among children on the spectrum. Many autistic children obsessively line things up, stack them, or put them in a certain order. Others adopt extremely specialized interests. One mother remembers, for example, her autistic son's obsession with microwave ovens. "He would draw them constantly—amazingly detailed drawings—he would talk about them constantly. He would pretend everything in the house was a microwave. . . . [He also] beeped like a microwave—constantly!"[9] Obsessions like these can last a lifetime, or they can come and go. If one obsession does wane, it is usually replaced quickly by another, which will be equally all-absorbing to the child until the next obsession comes along.

Resistance to any and all sorts of change is yet another common feature of autism. Children on the spectrum are often extremely attached to doing things in a precise way, at a precise time, with no variation. They may have rigid preferences for certain clothing, foods, and objects. If the routine does change, the child may become extremely distressed. Violent tantrums and meltdowns often follow, during which the child is inconsolable. Alternately, the child may try to physically bolt from anything new or different.

Social Skills

Not surprisingly, behaviors like these can contribute to social difficulties. Children on the spectrum often have trouble with the free-form ebb and flow of neurotypical interaction. They may shy away from it. Alternately, they may try repeatedly to engage with their peers but fail due to their poor social skills.

There are several key deficits in the social skills aspect of ASD. One is trouble with what scientists call social cognition. This term refers to the mental processes involved in perceiving, paying attention to, remembering, thinking about, and making sense of the people in one's social world. Children on the spectrum often have difficulty, for instance, understanding other people's perspectives and feelings. They also tend to miss nonverbal cues and misinterpret facial expressions and gestures. As a result, they may mistake people's intentions and meaning, respond inappropriately, or say unintentionally thoughtless and hurtful things.

Children on the spectrum are also frequently deficient in social reciprocity, which is the ability to have a back-and-forth interaction with other people. They tend to have trouble initiating contacts in a socially appropriate way. They may also have trouble responding appropriately if someone else initiates an exchange. Once a social interaction does begin, the ASD child may struggle to maintain proper turn taking in conversation—interrupting, losing the thread of the conversation, interjecting nonrelated ideas, and so on.

Lack of eye contact can be another problem. Many ASD children have difficulty making and maintaining eye contact with a

Many children with ASD have difficulty making eye contact with a conversational partner. This can make them seem cold and unfriendly.

conversation partner. This habit can make them seem cold and unfriendly. On the other side of the coin, some children have the opposite problem: They become overly friendly and stand too close, or they touch their conversation partner inappropriately. Because the child does not pick up on the other person's nonverbal discomfort—clues such as backing away or looking aside—he or she may persist, to the point of making the interaction very uncomfortable for the neurotypical person.

Sensory Processing Issues

For many people with autism, difficulties with communication, behavior, and social skills stem partly from sensory processing issues. These issues arise from the brain's atypical wiring, which causes the autistic person to perceive things differently from the neurotypical population. Almost all ASD sufferers have some type of sensory processing problem, although the specifics vary widely from person to person.

Oversensitivity is the most common perception problem in ASD. People on the spectrum may hear every tiny noise in their environment, to the point of constant distraction. They may find lights too bright, touch and tastes too intense, and odors overwhelming. One person with autism explains how oversensitivity affects her perceptions:

> For many people, the brain naturally sifts and separates visual, auditory, olfactory and tactile information. Your brain is able to decipher and discern what's important to focus on and set aside that which is less relevant at the moment. In my experience with autism, *everything flows through with equal force.* Life is like a continual sensory storm. . . . Everything hits me full on, and I've had to learn to sink or swim against the surging onslaught of my five senses.[10]

Undersensitivity is an opposite but equal problem for others on the spectrum. Children with autism may have an impaired ability to feel things that touch them, hear noises, taste food, and so on. For these individuals, it is like the world's volume has been turned down.

"In my experience with autism, everything flows through with equal force. Life is like a continual sensory storm."[10]

—Autistic woman

Some children on the spectrum experience a condition called synesthesia. In these individuals, the neurological wires are "crossed" so that one sense is experienced as another. For instance, the person may hear colors or feel the texture of words. One writer describes her experience of gaze as touch: "An eye 'touch' is what it felt like, and it was incredibly uncomfortable—it was moist and squishy and made my skin crawl."[11] Not surprisingly, this person avoided making eye contact with others at all costs.

Other Disorders

The many specific issues of autism are overwhelming enough on their own. But to make matters even worse, additional medical and mental health issues often occur alongside autism. They create another layer of difficulty for individuals on the spectrum to cope with.

On the mental health front, anxiety and depression are very common in ASD. One study suggests that up to 84 percent of children on the spectrum have clinical anxiety (anxiety severe enough to warrant a medical diagnosis) and up to 58 percent have clinical depression. There is no clear answer about whether these conditions are wholly biological or whether they result from the daily stress of autism, but most researchers believe both factors play a part.

On the medical front, seizure disorders such as epilepsy are the most common co-occurring ailment with ASD. Up to 39 percent of children on the spectrum have seizures or seizure-like brain activity. Tuberous sclerosis, a condition in which nonmalignant tumors grow in the brain and other vital organs, affects up to 4 percent of those on the spectrum. Gastrointestinal issues such as chronic diarrhea, celiac disease, and irritable bowel syndrome are also common, potentially affecting more than half of all ASD children.

Yet another slate of disorders falls more into the functional and behavioral realm. Children with autism are disproportionately likely, as a group, to suffer from attention-deficit/hyperactivity disorder, learning disabilities, and intellectual disabilities. Because these disorders often have symptoms similar to autism, it can be difficult to distinguish them. An ASD child's diagnosis, therefore, is often a tangled web of causes and effects, with much uncertainty about exactly which conditions are causing which symptoms.

Autism Outlook

With so many factors to juggle, autistic youth face an uphill battle in life. The difficulty of this battle is different for every person. A child with low-functioning autism will need support forever and probably will never live independently. For those with high-functioning forms of autism, the outlook is much brighter.

Still, there is no getting around the fact that falling anywhere on the autism spectrum poses a significant challenge for individuals who receive this diagnosis. But scientists are learning more about autism all the time, and society at large is becoming more educated and accepting of this disorder. With early diagnosis and the proper support from family and medical professionals, those on the spectrum have the best possible chance of living happy, productive, and independent lives.

Chapter 2

What Causes Autism?

Writer Carrie Cariello has learned to live with her son's autism diagnosis—most of the time. Some days, though, she feels wracked with self-doubt. She thinks about the long list of things that people have mentioned as possible autism causes, and she berates herself for not addressing each and every one of them. "Maybe I should stop using Tupperware . . . and re-paint the house to make sure there is no lead on the walls or the windowsills. Maybe I should throw away our frying pan. Maybe I should have loved him harder, deeper, more when he was a tiny swaddled baby squirming in my arms. Maybe this is my fault,"[12] she says miserably.

The feelings that Cariello expresses are not unusual for the parents of autistic youth. People often fear they are partly or wholly to blame for their child's condition. They are desperate to know what caused the child's disorder, and they spend their lives searching for answers to this question.

These answers, unfortunately, are proving to be elusive. Many environmental autism causes have been suggested—plastic containers, lead paint, cookware coatings, and poor maternal bonding, for example, which prompted Cariello's comments. Genetic

"Maybe this is my fault."[12]

—Carrie Cariello, mother of a child on the spectrum

and developmental causes have also been studied extensively. At this point, few definitive answers exist. Scientists do understand, however, that many factors play some part in causing autism. They also understand the disorder itself quite well from a physical perspective. They hope that knowing how autism works will eventually help them pinpoint its causes.

The Normal Brain

Autism is a disorder of the brain and nervous system. To understand how it affects a person's physiology and function, it is first important to understand the normal brain.

The brain is an organ that rests inside the skull. It is the controlling part of the nervous system, which is a network of nerves carrying information to and from the other parts of the body. Messages travel constantly through this network to control a person's movement, senses, bodily functions, reflexes, and countless other things.

The brain itself contains about 100 billion nerve cells. These cells are called neurons, and they are organized into regions that have different functions. A region called the cerebellum, for example, handles fine motor control, balance, and coordination. The occipital lobe controls vision. The frontal lobe takes care of many cognitive tasks, such as concentration, planning, problem solving, and speech; it is also largely responsible for personality. The amygdala processes emotions, particularly those related to fear or threats from the environment. These regions and others work together to control every aspect of a person's activities, thoughts, and feelings.

At birth, the brain's regions are not fully developed, but they progress rapidly. Scientists estimate that over 1 million new connections form every second between the neurons in a baby's brain. This process continues for the first few years of life to create an explosion of neural pathways. Once the pathways have formed, the brain then goes to work pruning them down to become more efficient and faster. Connections between the regions are maintained so the child's brain can communicate with itself—a bit like different departments working together in a corporation. This communication is coordinated so that the parts act as a team, helping the person function properly on a daily basis.

Information Flow

All of this communication is done in the form of electrical impulses that travel along and between neurons. The neurons are specially structured to handle this task. They are long and thin—up to 3 feet (91.4 cm) long in some cases. At one end of the neuron sits a

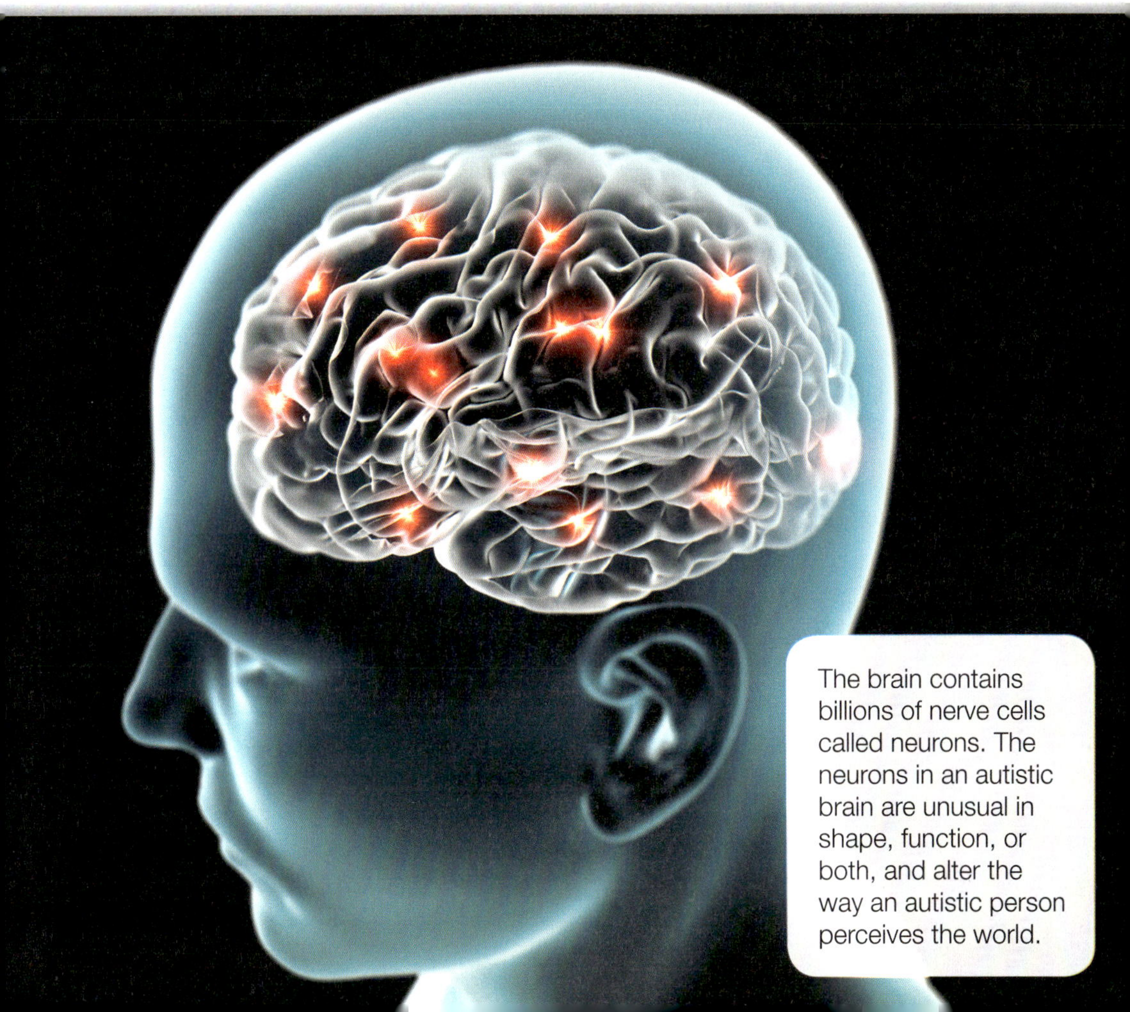

The brain contains billions of nerve cells called neurons. The neurons in an autistic brain are unusual in shape, function, or both, and alter the way an autistic person perceives the world.

cell body called a soma, which is fringed with hairlike projections called dendrites. A long, slender structure called an axon extends out of the soma. At its far end, the axon branches out into more fringes called axon terminals. The axon terminals of one neuron sit close to the dendrites of another neuron in an area known as a synapse.

The individual neurons' parts do not actually touch. Axon terminals are equipped with about fifty different chemicals called neurotransmitters that bridge the gaps. Depending on the message being sent, a terminal sends out the appropriate combination of neurotransmitters. These chemicals cross the synapse and enter receptors on the dendrites of the next neuron. This

Do Immunizations Cause Autism?

Autism usually becomes evident within the first few years of a child's life. This is the same time period when children are receiving routine immunizations. This coincidence of timing has led to a very vocal movement claiming that immunizations actually cause autism. According to this viewpoint, a too-fast flood of immunizations over the course of a few years may damage the child's developing immune system. Thimerosal, a preservative used in certain vaccines, has also been singled out as a potential autism trigger. The measles, mumps, and rubella (MMR) vaccine has also come under fire.

Study after study has looked into these possible links—and study after study has found that such links do not exist. On its website, the American Academy of Pediatrics maintains a database of more than forty such studies "to allow parents—and all those who administer or recommend vaccines—to read the evidence for themselves. These studies do not show any link between autism and MMR vaccine, thimerosal, multiple vaccines given at once, fevers or seizures," the academy states.

Still, the controversy continues to simmer, and some parents refuse to have their children immunized due to autism concerns. This trend has led to a resurgence in certain childhood diseases, particularly measles, mumps, rubella, polio, and whooping cough. Combined, these illnesses kill hundreds of thousands of children each year—an outcome that could be prevented by a single, safe pinprick.

American Academy of Pediatrics, "Vaccine Safety: Examine the Evidence," January 26, 2017. www.healthychildren.org.

input causes the neuron to fire an electrical signal, which travels through the axon to the next neuron. This process is repeated over and over until the message reaches its intended destination.

As the signal moves on from one terminal to the next, the synapses reset themselves in preparation for the next message. The neurotransmitters, having done their job, drift back into the space between the neurons. Some of these chemicals are picked up by structures called transporters, which return the neurotransmitters to their original axon terminals for reuse. Other neurotransmitters are destroyed by chemicals called enzymes. These processes go on constantly, and they are essential to the body's proper function. Dr. Shigeki Watanabe of Leica Microsystems in Zurich, Switzerland, explains that without prompt neurotransmitter recycling, "you would deplete all the [chemicals] from the terminals. Under normal conditions you wouldn't be able to think or move anymore in a few seconds. But obviously that's not what happens."[13]

Neuron Malfunctions

Watanabe describes the action of a normal brain. In the autistic brain, however, conditions are not normal. The neurons are unusual in their shape, function, or both. These changes can have a profound effect on the way the brain and the body work and, in return, on the way the person functions and perceives the world.

An alteration in a person's neurotransmitter balance is one irregularity often seen in autism. Studies show, for instance, that individuals with autism often have either too much or too little serotonin, a neurotransmitter that affects perception, memory, learning, and mood. They often have too much dopamine as well. This neurotransmitter affects sensory perception. In excess, it causes the mind to race and creates a condition of sensory overload that is typical of ASD.

Recent research is focusing on a link between autism and excess amounts of a neurotransmitter called glutamate or glutamic acid. While the effects of this imbalance have not been proved, scientists are studying many possible links. Increased glutamate has been suggested as a cause of seizure activity, which is common in ASD. Glutamate is also important for maintaining functions such as memory, learning, behavior, and motor activity. It is logical to believe, according to one study, that "abnormal glutamate levels might be associated with a wide variety of neurobiological and behavioral alterations in ASD."[14]

> **"Abnormal glutamate levels might be associated with a wide variety of neurobiological and behavioral alterations in ASD."[14]**
>
> —Study published in 2016 in *PLOS ONE*

Many other nervous system irregularities are seen in ASD. Individuals with this disorder often have reduced amounts of chemicals that control message flow through the synapses. This can cause the synapses to stay turned on for longer than they should, leading to various physical and mental effects. The neurons themselves may also be malformed. They may have too many or too few dendrites, or the axons may be atypical in shape. Even the distribution of neurons may be unusual in ASD, leading to changes in the shape and size of parts of the brain. All of these factors, both individually and together, affect the way a person functions.

Environmental Triggers

Although scientists understand how autism works from a physiological perspective, they are not certain what causes a person's neurons to malfunction or become deformed in the first place. A large number of studies have attempted to tackle this question. Many of them have focused on environmental triggers, which are things a child experiences or is exposed to in his or her surroundings. These studies have found quite a few things that may contribute to autism.

Influences that occur during pregnancy and birth seem to be the most likely autism triggers. Advanced parental age is linked to autism—the older the mother and father, the higher the risk. Certain illnesses in the pregnant mother, particularly measles, increase the risk of autism. The babies of women who ingest alcohol or narcotics during pregnancy have an increased risk of autism as well. A drug called valproic acid, which is used to treat epilepsy in pregnant women, has been linked to an increased risk of autism in the baby; so has terbutaline, which is used to stop premature labor. Still other risk factors include premature birth (before thirty-five weeks of fetal development) and oxygen deprivation during the birth process.

After birth, some substances in the environment seem to have an effect on the baby's likelihood of developing autism. The top suspects include certain pesticides, chemicals called phthalates (which are commonly found in plastics), industrial chemicals called PCBs, air pollution, and toxic waste. Exposure to any or all of these things may kick-start abnormal neuron development, which in turn may lead to autism.

Along with these findings, scientists have also ruled out some environmental factors once thought to play a role in ASD. These include diet, immunizations, and bad or emotionally distant parenting. All of these things have been studied extensively and been found to have no relation to the incidence of autism.

Links to Disorders and Illness

Childhood disorders and illnesses are other factors that have received close attention as possible autism triggers. There are well-documented links between ASD and certain disorders, particularly cerebral palsy, a neurodevelopmental disorder that affects body movement, muscle control, muscle coordination, muscle tone, reflex, posture, and balance. Muscular dystrophy, a condition that causes the muscles to weaken gradually over time, is also associated with autism.

Certain viral infections may also increase the risk of autism. Childhood measles and mumps are included in this group. So is encephalitis, an acute inflammation of the brain that can be caused either by viruses or by the body's immune system mistakenly attacking itself. This illness can permanently damage neurons and their synapses, possibly leading to the development of autism.

These links have not been definitively proved, and some scientists say they do not exist at all. A 2010 survey of 1.4 million children found that those hospitalized for *any* reason were more likely to receive an autism diagnosis at some point—but viral infections did not seem to carry an increased risk. For this reason, the study's authors concluded that childhood illnesses could not be considered a cause of autism. This result and others are still under investigation, and future findings may shed more light on this issue.

The Genetic Role

In many—perhaps even most—children with ASD, none of the known environmental triggers or other childhood disorders and illnesses seem to apply. For this reason, scientists have turned their attention to the possible role of genetics. After decades of study, the evidence suggests that genetics do indeed play a strong role in the development of autism.

The study of genetics is based on the makeup of a person's deoxyribonucleic acid (DNA), a chain of molecules that acts as the body's instruction book. It contains all the information the person needs to develop, live, and reproduce. DNA can be further broken down into genes, which are small regions of the DNA that affect specific traits. For instance, a gene might control a person's eye color, height, blood type, or other physical characteristics.

Each person has between twenty thousand and twenty-three thousand genes. The vast majority of these genes are normal and healthy. Scientists estimate, however, that somewhere between one hundred and four hundred genes in each person are not normal. They mutate either before or after birth in ways that may

Autism Has a Strong Genetic Component

Although researchers have not identified all of the possible causes of autism, their findings show a strong genetic component to the disorder. A 2017 Norwegian study looked at all research on patterns of autism passed from parents to children. It found that genetics accounted for 90 percent of the way autism is expressed in each individual, and environment accounted for only 10 percent of an individual's risk. Comparing these figures to other common disorders shows that autism is the most heritable (genetically influenced) of all of the disorders included in this study.

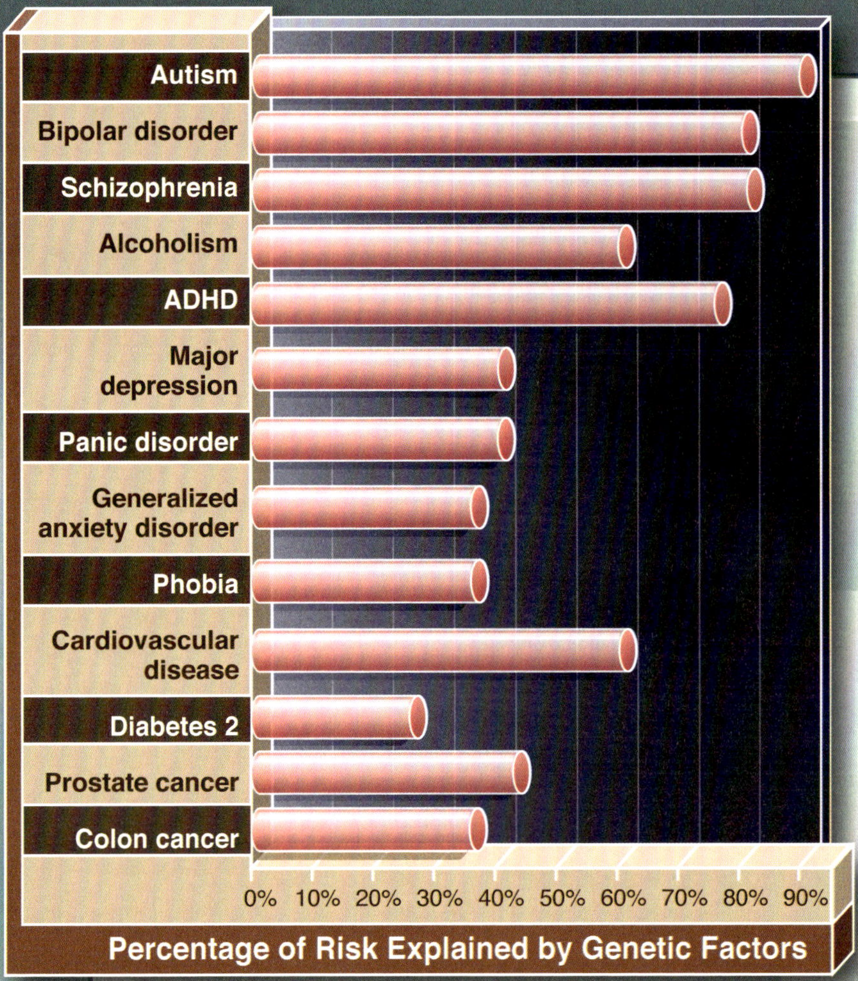

Source: Olav Bjerkehagen Smeland, "Analysis of Genome-Wide Association Studies Uncovers Genetic Loci Shared Between Schizophrenia and Cognitive Traits," 25th European Congress of Psychiatry, April 2, 2017, Florence, Italy. www.slideshare.net.

change their function and physiological effects. Most mutations are either harmless or suppressed by healthy genes. But some mutations in just a single gene can lead to devastating consequences.

Scientists have not been able to link one specific genetic mutation to autism. They have discovered, though, that many single-gene disorders do have effects that are very similar to autism. Fragile X syndrome, for example, results from a fragile area on the X chromosome and causes autism-like symptoms. Rett syndrome, Cornelia de Lange syndrome, and Down syndrome are other disorders whose symptoms overlap with those of autism. It is important to note that, as one scientist explains, "in most cases, when ASD characteristics have been described to be common in a syndrome, there are some subtle differences in the nature of

The Geek Syndrome

The so-called geek syndrome is a fascinating and controversial theory about the rising incidence of high-functioning autism in California's Silicon Valley. First proposed in a 2001 article, the theory states that adults with autism-like tendencies or undiagnosed Asperger's syndrome are disproportionately likely to enter technical fields such as engineering and computer science. In the course of their work, these people meet other like-minded people and form romantic connections. Because autism is highly heritable, children that result from these unions have a much higher-than-normal chance of being on the autism spectrum.

The reason this theory applies particularly to Silicon Valley involves the area's professional focus. Silicon Valley, which is a nickname for the southern portion of the San Francisco Bay Area in California, is an international hub for technical, scientific, and computer science organizations. Scientific studies show that there is, indeed, an increased level of childhood autism diagnoses in this region. Whether this result is due to autistic parents, however, is an open question. Scientists point out that autism is linked to higher education levels and increased parental age, both of which tend to apply to this population. Further time and study will be needed to determine whether the geek syndrome is real or just an interesting and coincidence-based idea.

these characteristics compared to individuals with ASD who do not have the syndrome."[15] The fact that the effects are so similar, however, suggests that genetic mutations probably play a role in autism as well.

Running in the Family

Evidence for a genetic link to ASD is further supported by statistical studies. Scientists called epidemiologists study populations or groups of people to look for medical patterns. Patterns of illness that run in families strongly suggest that certain disorders are heritable, which means they are passed on from parents to children through their genes—and autism shows a clear pattern of heritability. In fact, "The primary known risk factor for autism is family history," says Rebecca Landa, director of the Kennedy Krieger Institute's Center for Autism and Related Disorders in Baltimore. "Family history of an autism spectrum disorder can increase the risk for an autism diagnosis."[16]

> **"The primary known risk factor for autism is family history."[16]**
>
> —Rebecca Landa, director of the Kennedy Krieger Institute's Center for Autism and Related Disorders

Several important pieces of information support this conclusion. One is that autism is much more common in males than females. According to the CDC, autism affects 1 in 42 boys, but only 1 in 189 girls. This difference, which holds true across racial, cultural, and regional lines, suggests that autism has something to do with genetic differences between males and females.

Sibling studies provide another piece of the puzzle. According to some surveys, non-twin siblings of an autistic child have up to an 18 percent chance of being on the spectrum as well. This is twelve times greater than the risk in the general population and indicates a robust genetic connection for the disorder. The risk is about four times greater in male siblings than females, echoing the larger pattern of more boys than girls diagnosed with ASD.

Twin Studies

Twin studies provide even more convincing evidence for the heritability of autism. These types of studies are the gold standard for epidemiologists. They are based on the fact that identical twins share identical DNA, while fraternal twins are no more closely related than non-twin siblings. Both types of twins, however, did share the same environment and influences in the womb. When the twins are raised together, they also have a very similar postbirth environment and experiences. If significant differences exist in certain disorders between identical and fraternal twins, therefore, genetics are likely to be the primary reason.

Study after study has found that such differences do exist in autism. If one identical twin falls on the autism spectrum, the other twin has up to a 96 percent chance of being autistic as well. For fraternal twins, the numbers are much lower. If autism affects one fraternal twin, the other twin has between a 20 percent and 25 percent chance of also being on the spectrum—not dramatically different from non-twin siblings.

Some scientists have argued that correlations between autism in twins, either identical or fraternal, are due mostly to twins' similar upbringing and environment. But a recent analysis of all twin studies conducted to date used mathematical modeling to crunch tens of thousands of numbers. The incidence of ASD, conclude the study's authors, "is more consistent with strong genetic influences . . . [and] we can reject the claim that there is a strong shared environmental effect on autism spectrum disorders accounting for the majority of variance." At the same time, the authors say, "we *do not* exclude the possibility that environmental, or at least nongenetic, effects influence ASD. But unless a suitably powered and well-designed new study comes forward, this claim should be put to one side for now."[17]

Studies of twins have provided strong evidence of a genetic link to autism. If one identical twin is autistic, the other twin has up to a 96 percent chance of also being autistic. For fraternal twins, the chance is much lower.

The Epigenetic Explanation

For now, perhaps, the idea can be set aside, but not forever. More and more, it seems clear that autism results from a combination of genetic and environmental influences. The study of this interaction is called epigenetics. An epigenetic view of autism states that a child is genetically predisposed to autism, but an environmental trigger is needed to activate the disorder. This activation is thought to occur when outside influences modify certain chemicals, or "markers," that surround a gene's DNA. The modified markers do not change the gene itself or the underlying DNA sequence, but they do change the way the gene functions—for instance, by making the gene more or less active than it would normally be.

Epigenetic changes occur in all living organisms, not just people, and they vary widely in their effects. These changes can help or hurt an organism. They can also occur without having any obvious effect on the organism's overall health. In the case of ASD, epigenetic changes—if indeed they are occurring—seem to have impacts ranging from mild to catastrophic.

The impact level may relate to the amount of DNA affected. One example now being studied is a process called DNA methylation, an activity in which chemicals called methyl groups bond to the DNA strand. These bonds silence the expression of certain genes. In the case of autism, Shanghai Medical College of Fudan University physician Li Yu notes, "It could be that genes associated with neurologically-protective or regulatory pathways are silenced, and the more of these sites that are methylated or silenced, the more severe the symptoms of ASD would be."[18]

If scientists understood exactly which genes were affected in this manner, they might be able to reverse or at least stop the methylation process. But the answer is not that simple. Around one thousand genes are now associated with the development of autism, and although some seem more closely linked to ASD than others, the lines of causation are not clear. Environmental factors, too, are not well understood, and no single trigger has been pinpointed as the primary cause of autism. It is likely that genetic and environmental factors combine and interact in complex ways to affect a child's neurological development, immune function, and other factors, leading to the development of autism.

Different for Everyone

Another problem with understanding epigenetics is that every individual is different. One person, for instance, may be extremely sensitive to air pollution but have no dietary problems. Another person may cope just fine with air pollution but may be strongly triggered by the chemicals in plastics. A third person may have trouble digesting dairy and wheat products. The possible combinations of inborn sensitivities are endless. Add in the fact that each individual's environment is different as well, and what remains is a tangled, overwhelming mess of influences that may or may not lead to autism.

Untangling this web will take time and a great deal of continued research. Indeed, the causes of autism are so complicated that they may never be completely understood. But because autism is so prevalent, it is guaranteed to keep attracting the attention of the scientific community. As long as this disorder continues to strike the world's children, the search for answers will continue.

Chapter 3

What Is It like to Live with Autism?

Nancy is a young adult with high-functioning autism. Diagnosed as a child, she has learned over decades to manage her condition quite well. She is married, with a young son, and she holds down a full-time job. Most of the time, she says, "people do not notice my autism. I'm pretty good at faking it." But if people push Nancy past her emotional or physical comfort level, she loses control of the situation. She explains, "I start to revert back and the autism comes seeping out. I twitch, my leg will bounce, I can't look at people, and if I keep being pushed I usually end up banging my head on things and trying to get away from the situation by hiding somewhere quiet, cramped and dark."[19]

Jason, too, has learned to live with his autism—but for him, managing sensory input is the greatest challenge. He explains:

> A club is a nightmare, way too loud and too many people and lights. On the flip side when it's super quiet my mind focuses on the background hum, equally distracting. . . . Day to day life is just a lot of info input and I need some

time alone so my mind can process it all and dump the useless garbage. I'm fine as long as I don't go to intentionally overstimulating places and make sure I get enough rest.[20]

These two stories barely scratch the surface of what it is like to live with autism, since every person experiences this disorder a little differently. All people on the spectrum have processing difficulties that make life challenging even under the best of circumstances. With the right strategies, however, a person can learn to work around many symptoms of autism.

Too Bright, Too Loud, Too . . .

Sensory processing problems, as in Jason's case, pose a huge challenge for many young people with autism. Faulty wiring in the brain can make the world seem much too bright or too loud. Tastes and smells may be overpoweringly strong. The gentlest touch can be painful. These types of sensations are particularly hard for young children to understand and manage, and they can very quickly lead to an overwhelmed, agitated state. Adults with autism tend to manage these feelings a bit better than children do, since they have learned coping strategies over time. But even for adults, sensory integration problems can be overwhelming.

> **"People do not notice my autism. I'm pretty good at faking it."[19]**
>
> —Nancy, young woman with autism

A woman named Lori explains her auditory issues. "I hear your hair move in the wind (no, really, I do!), and it crinkles and tinkles in my brain. In the core of my being I feel you chewing your food at another table at the far end of the restaurant, and it makes it hard for me to swallow. . . . Every ounce of every inch of my body is continually battling this. It is undoing. It is unrelenting."[21] For Lori and others with auditory issues, avoiding loud environments is not just a preference, it is an essential survival strategy.

Extreme sensitivity to touch is another example of a sensory processing problem that affects many people on the spectrum. Children with touch sensitivity often struggle to avoid physical contact in ways that seem very frustrating and confusing to parents. A child might insist, for example, that all tags be cut out of clothing or might refuse to wear certain items because of the way the fabric feels. He or she might resist hair combing or teeth brushing because the sensations are so uncomfortable. The child might only be able to tolerate food with certain types of textures—for instance, crunchy versus smooth or hard versus soft. These types of strategies are the child's way of coping with an overwhelming flood of sensory input.

No Flexibility

Perhaps not surprisingly, sensory difficulties can lead to a very rigid way of coping with the world. Children on the spectrum may feel threatened most of the time, as if they are living in survival mode. They are constantly nervous that a sudden wave of sensory overload might overtake them. To avoid this potential onslaught, they develop a system of safe places and routines. They know from experience that any deviation can have painful consequences, so they stubbornly resist any type of change.

Sensory issues are not the only problem. Depending on the child's symptoms, many situations can feel unbearably threatening. A boy who is fixated on arranging toy cars, for instance, might not be able to stand the idea of being separated from this activity for an extended period. He might throw a tantrum when asked to run a quick errand with his mother. Or a girl who has poor communication skills might be terrified to visit the doctor's office because she knows she will be expected to speak to medical personnel. As a result, she may be very resistant to any type of medical care.

This lack of flexibility can be very difficult for neurotypical parents, siblings, and other people in the autistic child's world to understand. It does not seem like a big deal to these people to

Sensory processing problems pose a huge challenge for many young people with autism. Faulty wiring in the brain can make the world seem too bright or too loud.

try a different restaurant, chat with strangers, take a spontaneous stroll through a park, pet a strange dog, and so on. They often feel frustrated when the autistic child resists any and all new experiences. To the child, though, these things can feel like a matter of life or death. As one autistic adult explains it, "Trying to keep everything the same reduces some of the terrible fear."[22] New things might possibly have intolerable consequences, so they are best avoided at all costs.

Intense Interests

The same pressures that cause a lack of flexibility can contribute to the intense interests so typical of autism. In some cases these interests function as a coping strategy. One young man with

Sesame Street's New Neighbor

In March 2017 a new Muppet made her debut on the popular children's TV show *Sesame Street*. The character's name is Julia. She is four years old, with red hair and green eyes. She likes to pick flowers and paint pictures. And she has autism.

Julia was originally developed as part of a book publishing program called See Amazing in All Children, which aims to give children with autism someone to identify with—and to provide a window into the ASD world for others. Sherrie Westin, an executive vice president at Sesame Workshop who oversaw the initiative, says the campaign quickly struck a chord. "One of my favorite stories is a mother who said that she used the book to explain to her child that she had autism like Julia. This became the tool for her to have a conversation with her 5-year-old daughter," Westin explains. "At the end her daughter said, 'So I'm amazing too, right?'"

Sesame Workshop executives believe that Julia's character will inspire similar positive conversations in families around the world. They hope Julia will also help neurotypical children understand what it is like to live with autism, which will encourage them to be more tolerant of their autistic peers. Just by being herself, this simple puppet is doing great things to raise autism awareness.

Quoted in David Folkenflik, "Julia, a Muppet with Autism, Joins the Cast of 'Sesame Street,'" NPR, March 20, 2017. www.npr.org.

Asperger's syndrome explains that his activity of choice helps him handle the stress of everyday life. "My mind was constantly whirring with thoughts, worries, and concerns. The time spent with my obsession was the only time in which I had a clear mind—it gave me that much sought-after relaxation,"[23] he says.

While this man enjoys his interests, that is not always the case. Some people on the spectrum feel that their thoughts and behaviors are out of control and distressing. A woman named Mary explains:

> Sometimes the degree to which I obsess can be terrifying and overwhelming. I can lose sleep and it makes my chest hurt and my heart pound. Sometimes I forget to do

important things like eating, drinking, and peeing because I'm too focused on my obsession. I talk about it nonstop and even though I know I'm talking too much and I know I'm being annoying I can't stop.[24]

For parents of children on the spectrum, coping with intense interests can be difficult and sometimes socially awkward. A child with a shoe fixation, for example, may spend all of his or her time at home playing with the family's shoes. The child's conversation, if he or she is verbal, may revolve around footwear. This behavior can be tolerated in private. But as one autism organization points out, "It's one thing to talk about shoes a lot, but it's quite another to grab them off people's feet on the bus, or to have a tantrum if you try to move [the child] along after five minutes gazing into the shoe shop window."[25] For the ASD child, interests like these can quite easily cross the line into uncontrollable obsession, which in turn can interfere with the tasks of daily living.

> **"Sometimes the degree to which I obsess can be terrifying and overwhelming."[24]**
>
> —Mary, young woman with autism

Physical Manifestations

The pressures of life on the spectrum can lead to physical manifestations. Many autistic children engage in repetitive self-stimulating behaviors that have a soothing effect. These so-called stimming behaviors may include arm or hand flapping, flinger flicking, rocking, jumping, spinning or twirling, head banging, or complex body movements. A child may also repetitively use an object, such as flicking a rubber band or twirling a piece of string. Or the child may repeatedly stroke a certain object or sniff something.

Stimming arises mostly from sensory struggles. For some children, these behaviors are an attempt to gain sensory input. For instance, rocking might stimulate the brain's balance center. Hand flapping and finger flicking may stimulate the senses of touch and vision. In exactly the opposite way, other children engage in stimming to reduce sensory input. For example, focusing on one sound can block out others when the child is in a loud, chaotic environment. In nearly all cases, stimming is a sign that the child is uncomfortable in some way and is trying desperately to soothe himself or herself.

> **"I really can't explain why I need to do these things. I just know that if I don't do them, I get really anxious and can't function."[26]**
>
> —Anonymous teenage boy with autism

One high school senior compulsively touches doors in a complicated pattern when he walks through them. He needs to go through his particular stimming ritual each and every time he enters or exits a room. He explains:

> I really can't explain why I need to do these things. I just know that if I don't do them, I get really anxious and can't function. It does make me act funny . . . and it would be nice to have better control. A big goal of mine is to be able to control my stims so that I can go to college. Being unable to get out of a room is going to be a problem if I am in a room of hundreds of people.[26]

For this young man, stimming does not merely attract embarrassing attention, it also interferes with his ability to achieve his life goals.

Melting Down

Stimming and other self-management techniques help autistic youth manage their emotions most of the time. Sometimes, though, the level of sensory input or the dynamics of a situation become overwhelming. When this happens, an out-of-control episode called an autistic meltdown may occur. During a meltdown a child may scream, throw things, sob uncontrollably, moan and rock, or go dead silent and retreat from the world. Nothing can console the child; time is the only cure. The episode must run its course and wind down on its own.

An autistic teen named Tiffany describes what a meltdown feels like to her:

> I lose my ability to think or process, and can only feel. And I feel *everything*. Every noise, every draft. I want to scream, and sometimes I do, just wordless screaming. And all the while I feel like I'm watching myself in third person, and that tiny part of my brain that is still capable of rational thought keeps thinking, "Why am I doing this? Calm down, control it!" But I can't control it.[27]

For Tiffany and others on the spectrum, episodes like these are terrifying and debilitating. They can seriously affect a child's day-to-day life.

Sometimes autistic children may have a sensory overload that can result in a meltdown. During a meltdown, a child may scream, throw things, or go silent and retreat from the world.

Autism experts emphasize that meltdowns are not temper tantrums. They are an involuntary response to unbearable pressure. "It is not bad or naughty behavior and should not be considered as such," states the United Kingdom's National Autistic Society. "When a person is completely overwhelmed, and their condition means it is difficult to express that in an appropriate way, it is understandable that the result is a meltdown."[28]

Most parents of ASD youth come to understand this, with time and experience. But the world at large is not usually so understanding. "Some of these kids 'look' like they are typically developing, so it's hard for an outsider to not judge a perfectly healthy looking 9-year-old girl when she is throwing what looks like a temper tantrum,"[29] explains one mother. Young children may not notice disapproving glances from the people around them, but parents do—and this constant state of judgment can be very difficult to live with.

Need for Structure

A highly structured schedule can go a long way toward preventing meltdowns. When a child knows exactly what will be happening during the day, he or she can mentally prepare for those things—school, doctor visits, meals, baths, and so on. This type of routine is so important to some children that it must be scheduled down to the minute. If a doctor visit is set for 10:00 a.m., for instance, the child may need to know that the family car will leave the driveway at precisely 9:47 a.m. He or she may become agitated if the parent suddenly decides to leave four minutes early to buy gas on the way.

For lower-functioning children who struggle with verbal communication, visual schedules can be a big help. A visual schedule uses pictures to represent activities. It might, for instance, have a picture of an egg for breakfast time, a swing set for a playground trip, a bell for school, a rubber duck for bath time, and so on. It is usually posted somewhere prominent in the home where the child can see it frequently. By looking at the schedule each morning, the child can fix a picture in his or her mind of the day to come. Preparing for the day reduces anxiety, which in turn reduces the chance of meltdowns.

Many ASD children struggle with transitions between one event and another, so they need their schedule to include ending times as well as beginning times. It may be hard for them to understand, for example, that if they need to leave the house at noon, they should start wrapping up a painting activity by 11:50. Rushing the process can be overwhelming and can lead to a meltdown that is miserable for parent and child alike.

Challenges at School

Parents can usually arrange the home environment to meet the autistic toddler's needs. Once a child gets old enough for school, however, the challenges of autism balloon quickly. The school

Autistic Savants

Some individuals with autism have extraordinary skills in certain narrow areas. These people are known as autistic savants. An estimated 10 percent of those on the spectrum have savant abilities, compared to less than 1 percent of the neurotypical population.

There are many forms of savant abilities. The most common ones involve mathematical calculations, memory feats, artistic abilities, and musical abilities. Autistic savants may be able, for instance, to instantly name the day of the week for any calendar date, even hundreds of years in the past. They may be able to memorize vast quantities of information, such as the order of playing cards in a deck—an ability famously featured in the 1988 movie *Rain Man*, starring Dustin Hoffman and Tom Cruise. They may paint enormously skilled images despite being legally blind or compose musical masterpieces without any training.

It is not known why some people on the spectrum have abilities like these. Some scientists speculate that the faulty wiring of autism can lead to incredible concentration skills that the neurotypical population simply cannot match. Whatever the reason, the phenomenon definitely exists—and it can be a true gift for those who experience it.

environment is bigger and much less structured. It is often loud, bright, and colorful. Each classroom is packed with children who, being young, are not necessarily well behaved or considerate of others. And the teachers, even if they understand autism, may not have the time to focus on one child's special needs. All of these things can pose incredible challenges for school-age children on the spectrum.

There are things that can help ASD children in mostly neurotypical populations. All public school systems are required to make special allowances and arrangements for children on the spectrum, depending on their symptoms. A child with auditory

Once a child is old enough for school, the challenges of autism quickly balloon. Autistic children are often overwhelmed by the large, loud, and less-structured school environment.

processing or attention problems, for instance, might be assigned a seat at the front of the classroom, where it is easier to hear and pay attention to the teacher. A child with verbal struggles might get extra time on tests, homework, and other assessments. In the United States, these services and others are mandated through the Individuals with Disabilities Education Act, a federal law that guarantees a free and appropriate public education for every person with a disability. This means that ASD students must be educated at no cost to their families, and the education must be appropriate for the child's age, ability, and developmental level.

In theory, this sounds good. The reality, though, is that public school systems are overburdened. They may agree readily to special services but then fail to provide them adequately. Parents may spend years struggling against the system before finally giving up and moving their children to private schools that specialize in meeting the needs of children on the spectrum.

Social Struggles

The ASD child who does remain "in the mainstream," as the neurotypical-oriented educational system is sometimes called, faces ongoing challenges getting along with other children. At a young age, unusual physical mannerisms and poor social skills may frighten the child's neurotypical peers. As the years pass, these things usually become merely annoying rather than frightening to others. Children on the spectrum can be perceived as different and odd, and they may end up getting teased or bullied. At the very least, they are often ignored and excluded. They may feel very isolated and have a poor self-image as a result.

A 2013 study published in the *Journal of Autism and Developmental Disorders* highlighted the extent of this problem. According to the study, nearly 40 percent of young adults with autism never saw friends. Half were not receiving any phone calls or being invited to activities, and 28 percent reported having no social contact at all.

To avoid this outcome, children on the spectrum are usually encouraged to improve their social skills through practice, one-on-one therapy, structured course work, social groups specifically for those with autism, and more. One popular technique called Social Stories, for instance, seeks to boost social skills by modeling situations and the appropriate responses in a story format. This technique and others can help the child learn how to fit in with others. Even youth who do successfully learn social skills, however, often complain that they are just going through the motions—they do not really get it. "I'm just a huge phony. I'm faking my interest and enthusiasm 100% of the time. I leave most social events exhausted," one teenage girl says. "But hey, at least I can say I'm a good actress."[30]

Dating and Marriage

Faking it does not tend to go over well when it comes to romantic relationships, which are built on intimacy and open, honest communication. Dating is therefore a major hurdle for most teens on the spectrum. It continues to be challenging into adulthood, when serious relationships and marriage become options.

The first problem is establishing a romantic connection in the first place. ASD youth often have trouble understanding the signs of interest or rejection in another person. "Trying to interpret the meaning behind the little gestures, the closeness, or lack thereof, the little lulls and crests of conversation—It's like trying to crack [a] code for me," says one young woman with autism. "Needless to say, I don't get many second dates."[31]

If a relationship does progress past the dating stage and into a longer-term connection, or even marriage, further complications await. Neurotypical partners often struggle to accept the autistic partner's quirks, need for structure, bluntness, lack of emotional connection, and other autism-associated traits. Because those on the spectrum often have trouble reading others' feelings, this area, too, can be a minefield of misunderstanding. Due to these difficulties and others, people on the spectrum date and marry much less frequently than the neurotypical population. One Canadian study found that just 32.1 percent of people with autism had ever had a romantic partner. Only 9 percent had married, compared to about 50 percent in the general population.

> "We can be challenging people to love . . . but we can also be very rewarding to love."[32]
>
> —Anonymous married man with autism

Some people with autism find relationship success by partnering with others on the spectrum. "We like each other BECAUSE we're different. We don't talk trivialities, we talk about things that mean a lot to us. We're quirky, we like quirky friends, we do things our way," explains one ASD man with an ASD wife. "We can be challenging people to love . . . but we can also be very rewarding to love."[32] For this couple and many others, autism is no roadblock to relationship success.

Moving into Adult Life

Struggles with romantic relationships are just the beginning for youth with ASD. As these young people move into adulthood, they face many other so-called adulting tasks that pose their own unique challenges. Going away to college, living independently, finding and keeping a job, self-support, and parenting can all be prohibitively difficult for people on the spectrum. Many ASD men and women, particularly those who are high functioning, do manage these things—but those who fall lower on the spectrum may not have the tools to succeed. One recent survey shows that more than half of all adults on the spectrum still live with their parents. Just over 20 percent hold down a paying job, and the average pay rate for those who do is just $8.10 an hour.

Statistics like these are terrifying for youth with autism and for their parents, too. But it is important for these youth to remember that statistics are just numbers. Autism is a spectrum, and outcomes for those affected by ASD are a spectrum as well. With perseverance and support, many children with autism can expect to live happy, productive, and fulfilling lives.

Chapter 4

Can Autism Be Treated or Cured?

Many childhood illnesses can be cured by a simple visit to a doctor's office. The doctor gives the patient a shot or prescribes a medicine. A few days or weeks later, the problem is gonc. And in the case of childhood diseases, many can be prevented with vaccines that are given when a child is young.

Autism, unfortunately, does not fall into either category. Despite decades of research, scientists have not discovered any way to prevent autism. They also have not found a cure for this disorder. They have found a few things that seem to help—in some cases. But as a special report on the WebMD site points out, "One thing that complicates autism research is that different autism spectrum disorders may turn out to have different causes, may respond better to different treatments, and, perhaps one day, will have different cures. Today, however, ASD has no known cause, no one-size-fits-all treatment, and no cure."[33]

The lack of a clear answer has led to an explosion of experimental treatments for autism. According to one source, over four hundred such treatments are available today. They range from extreme diets to vitamin supplements, medications, acupuncture, targeted sensory stimuli, and much more. There is no scientific evidence that any of these treatments work. What *does* seem to help is early detection and support for children with autism—the earlier, the better. Once a diagnosis is made, there are many interventions that can improve outcomes for those on the spectrum.

Developmental Screening

The first step in treating autism is detecting it. In an attempt to make this happen as early as possible, pediatricians carry out standard screenings with infants and toddlers. These screenings look for the telltale symptoms and signs of many disorders, including autism.

> **"ASD has no known cause, no one-size-fits-all treatment, and no cure."[33]**
>
> —WebMD, online health resource

Developmental screening generally begins in infancy. At a baby's nine-month checkup, the doctor might ask the parents questions about the baby's behavior and development. The doctor might play with the baby to observe behavior, movement, and vocal expression. In subsequent visits, as the child ages, the doctor will also observe patterns of speech and learning. A delay in any of these areas could be a sign of a problem.

Doctors pay particular attention to babies who are at higher-than-usual risk for ASD. Having a sibling or parent on the spectrum is a red flag, since autism runs so strongly in families. Other items of concern include preterm birth, low birth weight, oxygen deprivation during delivery, advanced parental age, and other known risk factors. When any of these things exist, doctors will look carefully for signs of autism in a baby or toddler. They may refer the child for more comprehensive testing if they see anything alarming.

Further Testing

Comprehensive autism testing is usually carried out by specialists, such as developmental pediatricians and child-specific neurologists, psychologists, and psychiatrists. Often these professionals will start with screening tools that assess the child's general behavior and function. Common assessment tools include the Ages and Stages Questionnaire, the Communication and Symbolic Behavior Scale, the Modified Checklist for Autism in Toddlers, and the Screening Tool for Autism in Toddlers and Young Children. Most of these assessments are parent-completed questionnaires, but some include observation of the child by the specialists.

Pediatricians carry out standard screenings with infants and toddlers to detect disorders such as autism. A doctor often will play with the baby to observe behavior, movement, and vocal expression.

If screening tools reveal worrisome results, the child may be referred for diagnostic testing. Diagnostic tools rely on two main sources of information, the first being parents' or caregivers' descriptions of their child's development. This information is gathered in an interview format using a form called the Autism Diagnosis Interview–Revised (ADI-R). To complete the ADI-R, parents verbally answer questions about their child's social interaction, communication and language use, and restricted, repetitive interests and behaviors. Similar questions are asked over and over again in slightly different language to discern significant trends in the child's behavior.

The second important type of information comes directly from the child. It is usually collected on an assessment called the Autism Diagnostic Observation Schedule–Generic. To complete this assessment, a trained professional spends one-on-one time with the child observing his or her social interaction, communication, play, and imaginative use of materials. For children who are capable of understanding and responding to verbal prompts, direct questioning may be used. Behaviors and responses are scored on a 0 to 3 scale, with 0 indicating a completely normal response and 3 indicating a significant abnormality that interferes in some way with the child's functioning. If the total exceeds a certain threshold, the child is diagnosed with autism, and he or she may be referred for additional support.

Occupational Therapy

Occupational therapy is one type of support a child with autism might receive. In relation to therapy, the word *occupational* does not refer to job skills. It refers to the basic areas of function necessary to be successful in everyday life, such as fine motor skills, speech, problem-solving abilities, social skills, and anything else a child may be expected to do each day.

Because the symptoms of autism are different for every child, an occupational therapist begins with an assessment. The therapist

What Are You Looking At?

Early detection and intervention are important in the treatment of autism. For this reason, considerable research has been done on ways to detect autism as early as possible. Scientists have found that infants' eye gaze patterns offer a useful clue.

Eye gaze research is based on the fact that babies tend to stare at human faces, if given the choice of several images. In a 2010 study, scientists showed infants side-by-side videos. One video showed moving geometric images; the other showed a child dancing and doing yoga. Computers tracked the infants' eye movements to see where they were looking. The study's authors discovered that if an infant looked at the geometric images more than 70 percent of the time, the probability of the child being accurately diagnosed with autism was a shocking 100 percent. The reverse was true of normally developing infants. Out of fifty-one normally developing babies, only one preferred the geometric images—not a 100 percent correlation, but close.

This study, and others that look for early autism markers, may be a lifeline for families and children affected by this disorder. Early interventions offer the best hope for improvement. Tools like gaze tracking can help medical professionals detect autism in infancy and take quick action to intervene.

observes the child to see whether he or she can do age-appropriate tasks such as getting dressed, playing a game, or using the toilet. The therapist may even have the child videotaped during school or at other times the therapist cannot be present. The therapist will take note of any areas of difficulty, such as attention span, transitions to new activities, responses to touch or other stimuli, motor skills, and aggression or other negative behaviors, and then formulate an individual plan to address these problem areas.

Occupational therapists often work with clients for years. They get to know each child under their care. With time, they can bring about remarkable transformations. Al Roker, a *Today* show anchor whose son has autism, spoke on air in 2015 about his gratitude for his son's occupational therapist, Lori. Roker recalls that at age two, "[my son Nick] had a lot of issues. He didn't talk. He couldn't walk. He had very low body core musculature. And you know, a lot of people were not positive about his outlook." After years of occupational therapy, however, Nick was so improved that he was able to earn a black belt in tae kwon do. "I can honestly say that Nick is where he is today because of [Lori's] help,"[34] Roker says.

Sensory Integration Therapy

While physical shortcomings are the most pressing issue for some children, like Nick, sensory problems are the biggest challenge for others. Up to 80 percent of all children on the spectrum have trouble in this area. Sensory integration therapy, a targeted subtype of occupational therapy, is designed to help these children.

To understand how this type of treatment works, it is helpful to first understand the process of sensory integration. This is a term scientists use to describe the brain's process of pulling together information from many senses to understand and interpret the world. "Basically everything we do requires sensory integration," explains occupational therapist Lorna Jean King. This normal process, she says, "can be missing or very badly organized in some people, notably autistic individuals."[35]

> **"Sensory integration . . . can be missing or very badly organized in some people, notably autistic individuals."[35]**
>
> —Lorna Jean King, occupational therapist

To boost the sensory integration process, a trained therapist exposes an ASD child to sensory stimulation in a structured, repetitive way. The type of exposure depends on the child's needs. A child who has an unusual touch sensitivity, for instance, might wear a compression vest for a short period each day. A child who struggles with balance might receive specialized training in this area. Over time, the brain adapts and becomes able to process these practiced sensations more efficiently. To make the process even more efficient, some therapists will prescribe a program called a sensory diet that should be followed at home. Sensory diets have nothing to do with food. They are groups of activities, specific to a child's needs, that can alleviate symptoms whenever they arise, with or without the therapist's help.

Sensory integration therapy is a bit controversial. A 2012 review of twenty-five studies found no scientific evidence that sensory integration therapy actually works. Other, smaller studies, however, have found some correlation between the therapy and improvement in the child. Whatever the truth of the matter, many parents swear that their children have benefited from sensory integration therapy, sometimes in dramatic ways. Supporters say that this type of therapy does not hurt and may help, so there is no reason not to try it—as long as the client is willing and able to pay for it.

Individual Counseling

For some children on the spectrum, one-on-one counseling may be helpful. A technique called applied behavioral analysis (ABA) is typically used for younger children or those who are not fully verbal. This technique is based on the principles of operant conditioning, which states that behavior can be changed through a system of reinforcement and punishment. In other words, the therapist rewards the child when he or she does something well or correctly, and withholds a reward in the case of negative behaviors.

A mother named Jennifer remembers the first time her autistic three-year-old daughter, Anna, met with an ABA therapist. Anna could not speak at that point, so the therapist used nonverbal prompts to get her to do certain things. Each time Anna succeeded, Jennifer recalls, "the therapist gave her one M&M. It was just like training a dog." At first Jennifer was dismayed by this approach. After a few sessions, though, she started to see clear changes in Anna's behavior. With time and continued work, Anna improved so much that now, Jennifer says, "I don't tell people about the autism unless they have a reason to know, and they usually can't guess."[36]

For verbal children and teens with high-functioning autism or Asperger's syndrome, talk therapy is often useful. In this type of interaction, a counselor sits with the patient and discusses problems. The counselor then helps the child develop solutions and coping strategies. Talk therapy cannot cure autism, but it can help the patient manage issues that arise from being on the spectrum, such as social isolation, loneliness, anxiety, depression, and stress.

Learning Support

One-on-one counseling is helpful, but a weekly or biweekly therapy session cannot solve all of a child's problems. Extra support is usually necessary in a wide variety of areas. To meet these needs, many autism support organizations and resources exist.

In many high-functioning individuals, poor social skills are the primary cause of daily distress. Dysfunction in this area can lead to bullying, isolation, trouble getting along with teachers, an inability to get or keep a job, and many other negative outcomes. Because this is such a problem area, many organizations offer specific help for social challenges. Young children may benefit from autism-specific play groups, summer camps, or social skills training groups. Teens and young adults can take advantage of similar groups that focus on more mature types of social interaction, such as eating out at restaurants or going to movies. Teen groups may also emphasize the development of "adulting" skills, such as grocery shopping, housework, banking, obtaining a state ID card or driver's license, and other tasks of daily living.

Depending on a child's circumstances and symptoms, special needs schooling can also provide essential support. Many autism-specific elementary, middle, and high schools exist. Other schools cater to a broader special-needs population, but they have training and experience in handling and educating children on the spectrum. Switching a child from the mainstream to one of these schools is an emotionally charged topic, with passionate opinions both pro and con, so making the move can be a very difficult decision for parents. Once the decision has been made, however, many parents describe it as lifesaving. "None of Henry's [public school] teachers had bad intentions, but none of them fully understood what Henry needed. And none of them had the courage to admit that the public system they were a part of wasn't working for my son,"[37] said one mother after removing her child with Asperger's syndrome from public school.

One drawback of private special-needs schools and programs is the cost. These resources are not free, like public school. But in the United States, a great deal of scholarship and grant money is available to children with an official autism diag-

Many autism-specific schools exist for children in need of more specialized attention and care. However, switching a child to one of these schools can be controversial.

nosis. By providing these funds, states meet their responsibility to provide an appropriate education to every child, regardless of his or her individual needs.

Other Therapies

Appropriate education, counseling, training, and therapies with a proven track record of success are the cornerstones of any autism support plan. Many parents, however, do not want to stop at this point. They seek additional therapies that may help their ASD children function better or, at the very least, feel better.

Music therapy is one option. With this type of support, the child interacts with a therapist by beating drums, playing instruments, or making other types of music. Supporters say that music activates a different part of the brain than speech, so music therapy has different benefits than talking—particularly in the case of nonverbal children. As Donna Murray, vice president of clinical programs at Autism Speaks, points out, "If you can engage a child with autism with something appealing like music, at a minimum, that's a great start for some sort of social interaction."[38]

> **"If you can engage a child with autism with something appealing like music, at a minimum, that's a great start for some sort of social interaction."[38]**
>
> —Donna Murray, vice president of clinical programs at Autism Speaks

Animal therapy is another popular approach. Animal therapy can be as simple as bringing a pet into the family, or it can be a structured program run by professionals who help ASD children interact with horses, dolphins, farm animals, and other friendly creatures. For many children on the spectrum, this type of contact is pleasing in a tactile sense, and it provides an experience of connection as well. "Animals can relate to these children. And these children, who have a hard time relating to peers, can really relate to animals,"[39] says Colleen, whose ten-year-old son enjoys regular animal therapy sessions.

Medication

Talk therapy, social skills training, and other forms of support are important for those on the spectrum, but they do not address the many medical issues that tend to occur along with autism. For these problems, medications can be very helpful.

Psychiatric drugs are probably the most common prescribed medications for ASD children. Antidepressants and antianxiety medications are particularly common, since those on the spectrum often struggle with depression and anxiety. These medications work by altering the balance of neurotransmitters in the brain. This improves the function of the synapses, which leads to an improvement in mood and overall outlook. There are dozens of antidepressants and antianxiety medications available, and they all work a little differently. Finding the right match for a child's specific neurological makeup can be challenging, and the process can require a period of trial and error. When the right combination is found, however, the improvement can be nothing short of miraculous.

There is evidence that psychiatric drugs can ease some of autism's behavioral symptoms as well as the emotional ones. A class of antidepressants called selective serotonin reuptake inhibitors, for instance, seems to make social interaction easier for some children on the spectrum. Another drug called naltrexone, which is usually prescribed to help with alcohol and drug withdrawal, seems to lessen self-injurious behaviors in severely autistic children. And the US Food and Drug Administration has approved two antipsychotic drugs, risperidone and aripiprazole, for the treatment of autism-related irritability. Any or all of these medications can provide relief for certain ASD children.

Psychiatric problems are not the only medical challenge for children with ASD. Autism is often accompanied by seizure disorders, digestive problems, and many other strictly medical issues. The proper medications and treatments for all of these things improve the child's health, which in turn can improve the symptoms of autism.

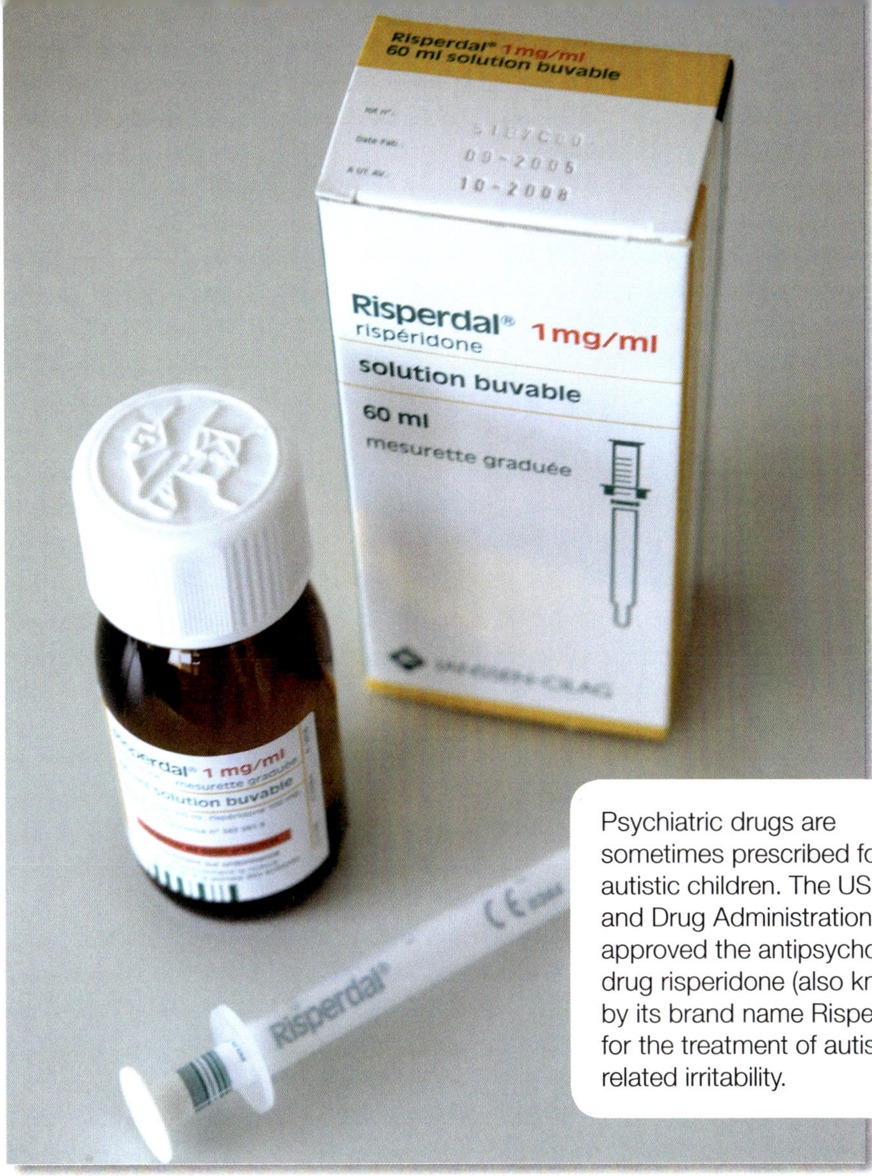

Psychiatric drugs are sometimes prescribed for autistic children. The US Food and Drug Administration has approved the antipsychotic drug risperidone (also known by its brand name Risperdal) for the treatment of autism-related irritability.

Gene Therapy

While medications mask the symptoms of autism, a field of study called gene therapy tries to reverse or stop the symptoms from occurring in the first place. Gene therapy is carried out with special cells called stem cells. Unlike most body cells, which have specific forms and functions, stem cells are unspecialized. They can develop into any type of cell the body needs. Scientists are trying to harness these cells to rebuild neural pathways in autistic children, leading to improved function and perhaps even a cure.

Temple Grandin

Diagnosed with autism as a young girl, Temple Grandin could not speak until she was almost four years old. With intensive therapy, she overcame her most severe issues. She went on to become an accomplished professional, a public speaker, and an ambassador for the autism community. In her classic book *Unwritten Rules of Social Relationships*, Grandin explains her path to success.

> Learning to be part of the social world around me is an ongoing process; I keep learning and doing better all the time. It's going to be that way for most kids on the spectrum; there's not a magic turning point after which things will become natural and effortless—it's a process.
>
> Medication was one of the things that made success possible for me, because it stopped the debilitating panic attacks. . . . For me, socialization is impossible if I constantly feel like I'm being attacked by a lion.
>
> To me, "success in life" is defined by my job, my friends, my contribution to society, not by becoming emotionally related so that feelings become my prime motivator.

Grandin's perspective has had a big impact on many people. She is comfortable with herself and with the way her mind works, and she does not feel she needs to be "cured." Successful just the way she is, Grandin is a strong voice for self-esteem and acceptance in the autism world.

Temple Grandin, *Unwritten Rules of Social Relationships.* Arlington, TX: Future Horizons, 2005, p. 378.

A 2017 study offers hope for this approach. Twenty-five severely autistic children received a transfusion of stem-cell-packed blood from their own umbilical cords, harvested at birth and saved for years in freezers. Each transfusion delivered up to 2 billion stem cells. Follow-up evaluations at six months and one year showed dramatic improvement in the children's autism symptoms. "Some children, who were not speaking very much, had big increases in their vocabulary and their functional speech," says Dr. Joanne Kurtzberg, the head of the medical center that ran the study.

"Many children were able to attend to play and have meaningful communication in a way that they weren't before. Some children had less repetitive behaviors than they did when they came onto the study."[40]

Kurtzberg and others involved in this study are quick to point out many potential flaws in their results. They particularly note that there was no comparison group of untreated children. Without a comparison, it is hard to know whether the treated children really did better than average or if their improvement was simply due to getting older. Researchers are now exploring this question through a second study, and they are very excited about the possible results. If transfusion proves to be much more effective than other therapies or no therapy at all, "we will consider that a breakthrough,"[41] Kurtzberg says.

Search for a Cure

Stem cell therapy is not the only attempt to tackle autism at the genetic level. Other ongoing efforts are trying to pinpoint and target the genes responsible for ASD in a variety of ways. One major push is being carried out by the organization Autism Speaks in collaboration with Google. Called MSSNG (pronounced "missing"), this project is collecting the genetic information of ten thousand autism-affected families and putting it online. To spur research, this database will be free to everyone, everywhere. "The greatest minds in science from around the world will be able to study trillions of data points in one single database. . . . [With] the help of the global science community we can far outreach what has been accomplished so far,"[42] explains the Autism Speaks website.

Results are already coming in. In 2016 Autism Speaks announced that researchers had used the database to identify sixty-one genetic variations linked to autism. Some of these variations were also linked to other disorders, such as heart defects and diabetes. By understanding these connections, medical professionals may be able to form better treatment plans for individuals on the spectrum.

Should Autism Be Cured?

The work of Autism Speaks, and other attempts to cure autism, have been the target of considerable controversy. Some people feel that autism is a difficult and sometimes crippling disorder and that a cure is desperately needed. Other people say that autism is not a disorder at all. It is merely a difference in brain wiring that should be understood and accepted, not viewed as a disability. The so-called autistic rights movement, which started in the late 1980s but picked up momentum in the first decade of the 2000s, is the primary purveyor of this message.

Many people refuse to support either side of the issue. They point out that the situation can be very different depending on where a child falls on the spectrum. For parents dealing with a nonverbal, self-harming, tantrum-throwing child who will never function independently, an autism cure probably seems like a welcome miracle. A high-functioning teen with a special musical or mathematical genius, on the other hand, might not only accept but welcome his or her place on the spectrum. This person might prefer to be accepted rather than cured.

The middle ground embraces both the search for a cure and the right to reject it. "We all need some tolerance for differing views," says John Elder Robison, a writer with Asperger's syndrome. "For example, I may see some benefits and some disabilities to my own high functioning autism. There are other people who see zero benefit and much handicap to autism in themselves. Both of us deserve the right to hold our differing opinions and live our lives in peace."[43]

This idea applies not just to those on the spectrum but to their families, friends, and other associates as well. There may never be a way to cure autism, but each family has the right to deal with it in the ways that feel most comfortable and are most effective for them. By taking advantage of proven therapies and techniques, ASD children can expect the best possible outcomes for their individual situations.

Source Notes

Introduction: A Global Epidemic

1. Quoted in Suzanne Murray, "My Autism Story: Cheryl's Daughter Amy Has High-Functioning Autism," CafeMom, April 14, 2010. http://thestir.cafemom.com.
2. Quoted in Murray, "My Autism Story."
3. Quoted in Alexandra Sifferlin, "This May Explain the Rise in Autism Diagnoses," *Time*, January 5, 2015. www.time.com.
4. Quoted in Sifferlin, "This May Explain the Rise in Autism Diagnoses."
5. Quoted in Autism Speaks, "Shift in Diagnosis Only Partly Explains Rise in Autism Prevalence," July 23, 2015. www.autismspeaks.org.

Chapter 1: What Is Autism?

6. Lori Sealy, "My Answer to the Question 'What Does Autism Feel Like?,'" Mighty, April 21, 2016. http://themighty.com.
7. Quoted in Merely Me, "Autism Awareness Month: Interview with Stephen Shore," HealthCentral, April 19, 2009. www.healthcentral.com.
8. Quoted in Autism Speaks, "Study Confirms 'Optimal Outcomes' Rare but Real Among Children with Autism," January 13, 2013. www.autismspeaks.org.
9. Brittany Miller, "Why It's OK My Son with Autism Is Obsessed with Microwaves," Mighty, September 4, 2015. http://themighty.com.
10. Sealy, "My Answer to the Question 'What Does Autism Feel Like?'"
11. Sealy, "My Answer to the Question 'What Does Autism Feel Like?'"

Chapter 2: What Causes Autism?

12. Carrie Cariello, "I Know What Causes Autism," Exploring the Colorful World of Autism, January 19, 2015. www.carrie cariello.com.
13. Quoted in Bernd Sägmüller, "Interview with Dr. Shigeki Watanabe on Research in Synaptic Membrane Dynamics," Leica Microsystems, July 7, 2017. www.leica-microsystems.com.
14. Zhen Zheng et al., "Blood Glutamate Levels in Autism Spectrum Disorder: A Systematic Review and Meta-analysis," *PLOS ONE*, July 8, 2016. www.ncbi.nlm.nih.gov.
15. Jo Moss and Chris Oliver, "Autism in Genetic Syndromes: Implications for Assessment and Intervention," Cerebra Centre for Neurodevelopmental Disorders, 2012. www.birmingham.ac.uk.
16. Quoted in Diana Rodriguez, "Who's at Risk for Autism?," Everyday Health, January 11, 2010. www.everydayhealth.com.
17. Beata Tick et al., "Heritability of Autism Spectrum Disorders: A Meta-analysis of Twin Studies," *Journal of Child Psychology and Psychiatry and Allied Disciplines*, 2016. www.ncbi.nlm .nih.gov.
18. Quoted in Kristen Hovet, "What Role Do Epigenetic Changes Play in Development of Autism?," Genetic Literacy Project, November 21, 2016. www.geneticliteracyproject.org.

Chapter 3: What Is It like to Live with Autism?

19. Quoted in Valkyrie_05, "Autistic People of Reddit, What Is Autism Really Like?," Ask Reddit, January 26, 2017. www .reddit.com.
20. Quoted in Valkyrie_05, "Autistic People of Reddit, What Is Autism Really Like?"
21. Lori Sealy, "A Cliffnote Confession from My Spot on the Spectrum," Mighty, October 17, 2016. www.themighty.com.
22. Quoted in National Autistic Society, "Obsessions, Repetitive Behaviour and Routines," October 11, 2016. www.autism .org.uk.
23. Quoted in National Autistic Society, "Obsessions, Repetitive Behaviour and Routines."
24. Mary Bey, "Do People with Autism Know That They Are Obsessive but Can't Stop Themselves?," Quora, April 8, 2017. www.quora.com.

25. Ambitious About Autism, "Obsessions and Special Interests," September 27, 2017. www.ambitiousaboutautism.org.uk.
26. Aaron Jepson, "Why I Stim," Jepson Files: One Family's Journey with Autism, May 16, 2016. http://jepsonfiles.com.
27. Quoted in Megan Griffo, "15 People on the Autism Spectrum Describe What a Meltdown Feels Like," Mighty, July 27, 2016. www.themighty.com.
28. National Autistic Society, "Meltdowns," March 9, 2016. www.autism.org.uk.
29. Quoted in Sheri Reed, "My Autism Story: Christa Has 2 Daughters on the Spectrum," CafeMom, May 7, 2010. http://thestir.cafemom.com.
30. throwaway5665326885, comment on marksun5, "People Who Have Good Social Skills and Used to Be Awkward or Bad Socially, How Did You Get Good Social Skills?," Reddit, 2017. www.reddit.com.
31. Megan Cramer, "What It's like to Date When You're on the Autism Spectrum," *Vice*, August 17, 2017. www.vice.com.
32. Anonymous, comment on Quora, "Do Autistic People Ever Get Married? What Are Relationships like with High Functioning Individuals with Autism?," October 25, 2015. www.quora.com.

Chapter 4: Can Autism Be Treated or Cured?

33. Daniel J. DeNoon, "Finding the Right Autism Treatment," WebMD, March 27, 2008. www.webmd.com.
34. Quoted in Eun Kyung Kim, "'A Godsend': Meet Lori Rothman, the Therapist Who Changed Al Roker's Son's Life," *Today*, December 17, 2015. www.today.com.
35. Quoted in Stephen M. Edelson, "Interview with Lorna Jean King, OTR, FAOTA," Autism Research Institute, June 9, 1996. www.autism.com.
36. Jennifer, personal communication with the author, April 17, 2017.
37. Amy Mackin, "How My Autistic Son Got Lost in the Public School System," *Atlantic*, January 3, 2013. www.theatlantic.com.
38. Quoted in Susan Scutti, "Study Casts Doubt on Music Therapy for Kids with Autism," CNN, August 8, 2017. www.cnn.com.

39. Quoted in Krisha McCoy, "How Pet Therapy Can Help Autism," Everyday Health, January 12, 2010. www.everydayhealth.com.
40. Quoted in Wayne Drash and Sanjay Gupta, "Stem Cells Offer Hope for Autism," CNN, April 5, 2017. www.cnn.com.
41. Quoted in Drash and Gupta, "Stem Cells Offer Hope for Autism."
42. Autism Speaks, "About—MSSNG." www.autismspeaks.org.
43. John Elder Robison, "The 'Cure' for Autism, and the Fight over It," *Psychology Today*, October 12, 2009. www.psychologytoday.com.

Organizations and Websites

Autism Science Foundation (ASF)

106 W. Thirty-Second St., Suite #182
New York, NY 10001
http://autismsciencefoundation.org

The ASF funds cutting-edge autism research. It also provides information about autism to the general public and supports the needs of individuals with autism. This website is a good place to find summaries of the most recent research and results.

Autism Society

4340 East-West Hwy., Suite 350
Bethesda, MD 20814
www.autism-society.org

The Autism Society works to increase public awareness about the day-to-day issues of people across the spectrum, advocates for appropriate services for individuals of every age, and provides the latest information regarding treatment, education, research, and advocacy.

Autism Speaks

1 E. Thirty-Third St., 4th Floor
New York, NY 10016
www.autismspeaks.org

Autism Speaks is dedicated to promoting solutions across the spectrum and throughout the life span for the needs of individuals with autism and their families through advocacy and support, increasing understanding and acceptance of people with ASD, and advancing research into causes and better interventions for ASD and related conditions.

Autistic Self Advocacy Network (ASAN)

PO Box 66122
Washington, DC 20035
http://autisticadvocacy.org

ASAN's motto is "Nothing about us without us." This organization is run by people on the spectrum, and it speaks from their unique points of view on issues relating to autism.

Center for Autism and Related Disorders (CARD)

21600 Oxnard St., Suite 1800
Woodland Hills, CA 91367
http://centerforautism.com

CARD is one of the world's largest organizations using applied behavior analysis in the treatment of ASD. Its website offers a significant amount of information on this effort.

Centers for Disease Control and Prevention (CDC)

1600 Clifton Rd.
Atlanta, GA 30329
www.cdc.gov

The CDC is America's most authoritative organization on diseases and disorders. Its website offers a wealth of information about all major health challenges, including ASD.

National Institute of Mental Health (NIMH)

6001 Executive Blvd., Room 6200, MSC 9663
Bethesda, MD 20892
www.nimh.nih.gov

The NIMH seeks to transform the understanding and treatment of mental illnesses. Its website offers information and education on a wide variety of mental health issues, including those that co-occur with autism. The website also addresses autism directly.

Siblings of Autism

40 West St., Annapolis, MD 21401
www.siblingsofautism.org

Siblings of Autism is dedicated to supporting the siblings of individuals on the autism spectrum through scholarships, respite funds, and outreach programs.

For Further Research

Books

Naoki Higashida, *The Reason I Jump: The Inner Voice of a Thirteen-Year-Old Boy with Autism*. New York: Random House, 2016.

Irene McHenry and Carol Moog, *The Autism Playbook for Teens: Imagination-Based Mindfulness Activities to Calm Yourself, Build Independence, and Connect with Others*. Oakland, CA: Instant Help, 2014.

Jennifer Cook O'Toole, *Sisterhood of the Spectrum: An Asperger Chick's Guide to Life*. London: Kingsley, 2015.

Barry M. Prizant, *Uniquely Human: A Different Way of Seeing Autism*. New York: Simon & Schuster, 2016.

The Students of Limpsfield Grange School, *M Is for Autism*. London: Kingsley, 2015.

Internet Sources

Ruth Padawer, "The Kids Who Beat Autism." *New York Times Magazine*, July 31, 2016. https://www.nytimes.com/2014/08/03/magazine/the-kids-who-beat-autism.html.

Lori Sealy, "My Answer to the Question 'What Does Autism Feel Like?'," Mighty, April 21, 2016. https://themighty.com/2016/04/what-does-autism-feel-like/.

Emily Shire, “Dating on the Autism Spectrum,” *Atlantic*, August 5, 2013. https://www.theatlantic.com/health/archive/2013/08/dating-on-the-autism-spectrum/278340/.

Maia Szalavitz, “Autism—It’s Different in Girls.” *Scientific American*, March 1, 2016. https://www.scientificamerican.com/article/autism-it-s-different-in-girls/.

Jim Walter, “This Is Why My Family Uses ‘Autistic,’” Healthline, September 26, 2017. https://www.healthline.com/health/autism/why-i-chose-autistic-as-a-label.

Index

Note: Boldface page numbers indicate illustrations.

Picture Credits

Cover: VStock/Thinkstock Images

6: Maury Aaseng
10: Juanmonino/iStockPhoto.com
15: Maury Aaseng
19: Photographee.eu/Shutterstock.com
25: Naeblys/Shutterstock.com
31: Maury Aaseng
35: News Syndication/Newscom
41: Photographee.eu/Shutterstock.com
45: japansainlook/Shutterstock.com
48: stockfour/Shutterstock.com
54: goodluz/Shutterstock.com
60: BSIP/Newscom
63: BSIP/Newscom

About the Author

Kris Hirschmann has written more than four hundred books for children. She owns and runs a business that provides a variety of writing and editorial services. She lives just outside Orlando, Florida, with her daughters, Nikki and Erika.